4/20/05

$15.50

DATE			

BAKER & TAYLOR

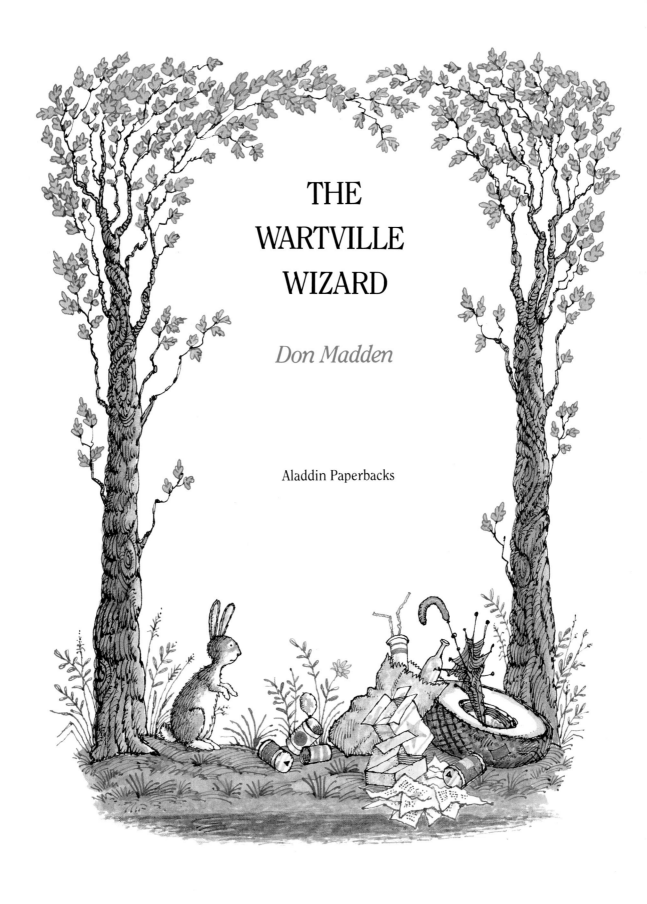

THE
WARTVILLE
WIZARD

Don Madden

Aladdin Paperbacks

Aladdin Paperbacks
An imprint of Simon & Schuster
Children's Publishing Division
1230 Avenue of the Americas
New York, NY 10020
Copyright © 1986 by Don Madden
All rights reserved including the right of reproduction
in whole or in part in any form.
First Aladdin Paperbacks edition, 1993
Printed in Hong Kong by South China Printing Company Ltd.
13 14 15 16 17 18 19 20
The text of this book is set in 13 pt. ITC Clearface.
The illustrations are rendered in pen-and-ink and watercolor and
reproduced in full color.

Library of Congress Cataloging-in-Publication Data
Madden, Don, 1927–
The Wartville wizard / Don Madden.—1st Aladdin Books ed.
p.   cm.
Summary: An old man fights a town of litterbugs by magically sending each
piece of trash back to the person who dropped it.
ISBN 0-689-71667-2
[1. Refuse and refuse disposal—Fiction. 2. Magic—Fiction.
3. Environmental protection—Fiction.] I. Title.
PZ7.M254War 1993
[E]—dc20   92-22246
ISBN-13: 978-0-689-71667-2

For
Marie Kennedy Madden,
a great mom
and
a great lady

The road to Wartville traveled over a hill. In a neat and tidy house on top of the hill lived a neat and tidy old man. This is the story of how he became known as the Wartville Wizard.

Every morning the old man looked out his window and watched the birds playing in the birdbath. He saw the flowers dancing in the sunlight and the trees waving in the breeze. From inside, it seemed a perfect place. But when he went outside, he saw that it was not.

Under the beautiful flowers he found soda bottles thrown from cars during the night. By the mailbox he saw juice cans, plastic cups, and straws. Along the road he spotted more litter: empty cigarette packs, newspapers, candy wrappers, all kinds of trash. Once he found a worn-out baby buggy full of pacifiers. Another day he discovered a broken toilet seat leaning against the garden gate.

Every day the old man became angry. The more trash he saw, the more angry he got. Sometimes he ran back to his house and up the stairs and leaned out his bedroom window. Taking a deep breath, he yelled, "The people of Wartville are *slobs*!"

Then the old man took a burlap sack from the garden shed and walked along the roadsides, collecting the trash.

Day after day, month after month, he trudged up and down the road with his burlap sack. Some days were not as bad as others, but there was always something to put into the sack. He knew if he stopped cleaning, everything would be smothered under a blanket of trash. "Slobs! Slobs! Slobs!" he grumbled.

One day the old man struggled up the hill with an extra heavy load. The afternoon before, the Senior Citizens Football Team and the Gourmet Motorcycle Club had held their annual picnics. What a mess!

When he got home, he emptied the sack into a big barrel and jumped up and down on top of the heap, squeezing the garbage so that nothing would fall out. But a plastic lid did fall out. HAVE A NICE DAY, it said.

The old man shook his head and walked slowly into the woods. He was tired of collecting, tired of pulling and dragging, tired of jumping up and down to make the barrel hold more—just plain tired of trash. It no longer helped to yell "Slobs!"

He stopped in a clearing in the middle of the woods and looked up at the treetops. Then he looked into the blue beyond and whispered, "Mother Nature, I've tried to keep your hill and green places clean, but I can't go on. I'm tired." He heaved a sigh and sat down on the ground.

Suddenly soft music played around the old man, and then all was still. Even the birds stopped singing, and the bushes and trees stopped rustling their leaves.

The old man let the quiet wrap around him like a cozy blanket. It was brief, but when it passed he knew he had been given *the power over trash*!

He felt calm and rested as he walked back to the road. A long, shiny automobile drove by. Out the back window a small hand tossed a candy wrapper into the air. It was a Cruncho Snuggles wrapper, and it fluttered to the side of the road and settled on a clump of dandelions.

The old man looked at it and frowned. He pointed his finger at it and said, "Go back and stick to the person who threw you!"

The wrapper wiggled. Then it shot up into the air and flew down the road after the automobile.

In the back seat, little Barbette Swartley felt something hit the side of her face. She reached up and found the Cruncho Snuggles wrapper on her cheek. She pulled it. It would not come off!

That night at dinner, Barbette wore a bandanna around her face. She said she was playing pirate. She didn't want her parents to see the wrapper, since she wasn't supposed to eat candy between meals.

The next morning, as usual, there was trash along the road. But the old man didn't use the burlap bag. He simply pointed at each can, bottle, box, or whatever litter, and sent it back to whoever had thrown it—exactly as he had done with the Cruncho Snuggles wrapper. It was certainly easier than dragging it all up the hill, and he felt happy.

But there were people in Wartville who were not happy.

Harvey Bender had just gotten home from work at the bathtub factory five miles out of town. As he stepped through his front doorway, an aluminum beer can hit him on the back of the neck—and stuck there!

Mr. Fullerton K. Hardboard, chairman of the Wartville Real
Estate Society, was startled when a damp, burned-out cigar
suddenly attached itself to his elbow!

And Mrs. Mabel Botts let out a piercing scream when a paper bag full of garbage chased her down the street and stuck to her rear end!

The only doctor in Wartville was Melvin Splint. That night there were a lot of people in his waiting room wearing strange outfits. They were trying to hide the things that were attached to them.

As the patients came into his office one by one, Dr. Splint began

to worry. "I have never seen anything like this," he said. "It may be an epidemic!" He told the people he would go to the next town and ask another doctor for advice. "Come back to see me tomorrow afternoon," he said.

The doctor passed the old man's house as he drove over the hill to the next town. He was worried about his patients. He opened a pack of gum and took out two pieces at once, throwing the gum wrappers out the window.

Dr. Splint did not learn anything from the doctor in the next town. But he did get something out of his trip. The next afternoon, when he opened his office door, the people in the waiting room gasped. They saw a gum wrapper stuck to each of his ears!

"Oh, my goodness!" said Fullerton K. Hardboard. The people went home. They were very depressed.

As the days went by, more and more townspeople began to wear strange outfits. One lady went to the market in a tent. When she was leaving, she met a friend wearing a quilted plastic garment bag. They got stuck trying to go out the door together. A sofa slipcover walked into the library and returned an overdue book. The librarian fainted. And down at the bus station a very upset sleeping bag and a large beach umbrella were seen leaving town.

Poor little Barbette Swartley was sick and tired of wearing the bandanna to hide the Cruncho Snuggles wrapper. She decided to go for a long walk. "When I get out of town, I'll be able to take this thing off for a while," she mumbled to herself.

Walking slowly along the road that traveled over the hill, she undid the knot and removed the bandanna. The Cruncho Snuggles wrapper crackled in the breeze. But the air felt good on her head.

Halfway down the other side of the hill, Barbette saw the old man looking for trash. She didn't want to be caught without her disguise, so she hid behind a bush and peeked out.

The old man had found a pile of empty soda cans, some Popsicle sticks, and a milk carton. He pointed his finger at each piece of trash and said something. Instantly the soda cans and Popsicle sticks and the milk carton jumped into the air and flew down the road to Wartville!

Barbette's eyes almost popped out of her head! She waited until the old man had gone into his house. Then she ran down the road as fast as her legs would carry her.

"He's a wizard!" she sputtered. "A wizard with power over trash! That's why things are sticking to everybody! He's a wizard!"

When the townspeople had heard Barbette's story, they decided to call a meeting. By this time almost every family in Wartville had been stricken, and some people were in really bad shape— especially Jimmy VanSlammer, who couldn't fit through the door.

Dr. Splint called the meeting to order. He asked the group to keep calm. While he spoke, the gum wrappers on his ears wiggled and waved.

The meeting lasted late into the night. The people wanted to

show one another the nasty trash they had been trying to hide. They were all relieved to know that others had the same problem.

The meeting was tiring for Mrs. Botts, the lady with the bag of garbage on her rear end, because she couldn't sit down. Finally Fullerton K. Hardboard stood up. "I move we adjourn the meeting and get some sleep," he said. "Tomorrow we'll go out to this wizard's place and demand that he remove these awful stick-ons!" Everybody agreed.

When the old man looked out his window the next morning, he saw cars and trucks pulling up and parking all around his house. Even the sheriff's car was there.

The old man stepped outside. He was glad to see that the sheriff wasn't wearing any garbage.

"These folks claim you're a wizard, mister," said the sheriff. "They say you made all this stuff stick to them. Let's hear what you

have to say about it. We're all ears."

Angry shouts and grumbling noises came from the crowd. Fullerton K. Hardboard boomed, "We demand action, sheriff!" Poor Mrs. Botts yelled, "Boo!" She was a nervous wreck from standing up so long.

The old man looked at the crowd with a serious, steady look, taking them in one at a time. Finally he said, "Hello, slobs!"

"Arrest him, sheriff!" shouted Harvey Bender.

The old man gave them another steady look. "You're angry because your trash has come home to you," he said. "You've been throwing trash along the road for a long time, and I've been cleaning it up. I'm tired of cleaning up after you. Every piece of trash stuck to you is something you yourselves threw away."

The grumbling and shouting changed to a murmur and then stopped. A hush came over the people.

Fullerton K. Hardboard studied the cigar butts that were stuck to him. Other people looked closely at their own stick-ons. They all began to feel embarrassed.

Suddenly a muffled whine came from Jimmy VanSlammer, who was getting desperate. "Suppose we promise not to do it again?"

Everyone looked at Jimmy. All they could see was a large pile of soda cans, Popsicle sticks, hamburger cartons, and candy wrappers, with two skinny legs sticking out underneath.

Then they looked at the old man. They weren't angry anymore. They were ashamed.

The old man smiled. He wasn't angry anymore, either. He knew they had learned a lesson. "If all of you promise not to litter again, and mean it," he said, "the trash will stop sticking to you when you get home. Then you can put it in your own trash baskets, where it belongs!"

The people rushed to their cars and trucks. "Maybe he's not such a bad wizard, after all!" someone shouted.

Little Barbette Swartley was so happy that on the way home she almost threw the bandanna out the car window. But she stopped herself just in time.

Mrs. Botts felt better, too. Unfortunately, though, she had to ride back the way she had come—standing in the back of a pickup truck with her garbage bag rattling in the wind.

Dr. Splint was glad the epidemic was ending. He opened a new pack of gum and carefully put the wrapper in his car's litter bag.

When all the people had gone, the old man walked along the road. The Johnny jump-ups were lifting their heads proudly, the wild geraniums were beaming, and everything was neat and tidy. He was happy because he knew it would stay that way. But he would miss yelling "Slobs!" a little, because that was kind of fun.